Devin & Goliath

Mary Blount Christian

illustrated by
Normand Chartier

Addison-Wesley

to my son, Devin
Mary Blount Christian

to Sandi
Normand Chartier

Young Scott Books
by Mary Blount Christian

Nothing Much Happened Today
Devin and Goliath

Young Scott Books

Text Copyright © 1974 by Mary Blount Christian
Illustrations Copyright © 1974 by Normand Chartier
All Rights Reserved
Addison-Wesley Publishing Company, Inc.
Reading, Massachusetts 01867
Printed in the United States of America
First Printing
GO/HO   9/74   01026

Library of Congress Cataloging in Publication Data

Christian, Mary Blount.
  Devin and Goliath.

  SUMMARY: A little boy catches a big turtle but re-
turns it to the pond when he discovers how unhappy the
animal is in captivity.
  [1. Turtles—Fiction]   I. Chartier, Normand,
1945-   illus. II. Title.
PZ7.C4528De   [E]   74-2089
ISBN 0-201-01026-7

Bit by bit
Devin crawled
through the wet grass.
Without a sound
he pulled back the tall weeds.
He searched the shallow creek.

There!
Now he could see him.
There was Goliath!
There was that old turtle!
He was sunning on a flat rock
in the middle of the creek.

His knees bent,
Devin crept into the shallow creek.
His movement barely
made the water ripple.
He was close to Goliath.

Suddenly the big turtle
slipped noiselessly
into the water.

In a second he was gone.
Devin made a last desperate grab
in the turtle's direction.
SPLASH!
He tumbled into the shallow water.

Devin went home
to change clothes.
He told himself,
"I've just got
to catch that turtle.
I've just got to!"

The next day
Devin returned
to the creek.
There was Goliath.
He was on his favorite rock.

Devin quietly eased
a piece of bacon
into the water where
Goliath would see it.
The meat was tied
to a long string.

Devin jerked the string.
The bacon wiggled.
The turtle cocked his head.
He tilted it this way and that.
Slowly Goliath slid into the water.
He glided toward the meat.

Just as he snapped at the meat,
Devin eased it out of Goliath's reach.
Again Goliath glided toward the meat.
Again he tried to snatch it.
Each time Devin pulled the meat away.
Goliath was so interested in
the meat that he was not careful.

Suddenly Devin grabbed Goliath.
The big turtle squirmed and kicked.
He could not get away from Devin.

At home Goliath
scratched and thumped
in a big box.
Devin was making a
cage in which to keep him.
When the cage was ready
Devin put Goliath in.

It had a pan with water
for Goliath to sit in.
It had a rock for him to sit on.
Goliath scratched and thumped.
He could not find a way out.

Devin's friends came
to see Goliath in his new home.

Each day
Devin took
food to Goliath.
In the beginning
Goliath tried to escape.

At last he just sat. He sat
in his pan of water.

As the weeks passed
Devin watched Goliath.
The turtle no longer
held his long neck
straight and high.
He looked somehow
smaller to Devin.

Devin thought about Goliath.
He didn't know what he should do.
Finally Devin put the big turtle
into a box.
He carried the box to the creek.
Devin took Goliath out.
He set him on the flat rock
in the center of the creek.

Goliath sat very still.
Then he stretched
his long neck.
He cocked his head
this way and that.

At last Goliath slid silently
into the shallow water
and disappeared from sight.

Devin picked up the box.
He slowly walked home.

Devin still goes to the creek.
Silently he creeps to the edge
and peers through the tall weeds.
And Goliath still suns
himself on the flat rock.
Devin now knows this is
where Goliath
belongs.